the Brollys

JACK FROST

Story by Shirley Isherwood
From an original idea by Stuart Kettle

BBC BOOKS

Published by BBC Books,
a division of BBC Enterprises Limited,
Woodlands, 80 Wood Lane, London W12 0TT
First published 1990
© The Weather House, 1990
Licensed by BBC Enterprises Ltd.
Illustrations by Stuart Kettle and Thomas Barker © The Weather House
ISBN 0 563 36086 0
Set in Century Schoolbook by Goodfellow & Egan Ltd., Cambridge
Printed and bound in Great Britain by Cambus Litho, East Kilbride
Colour separations by Dot Gradations, Chelmsford
Cover printed by Clays Ltd, St Ives Plc

Harry was trying to get to sleep. But no sooner had he closed his eyes, than he opened them again. On the wall hung his little Weatherhouse. If the day was going to be fine and sunny, Mrs Brolly came through her door. If the day was going to be wet, Mr Brolly came out. As Harry stared up at the Weatherhouse, his bed seemed to grow smaller and he found himself at the door of the little house on the wall.

When Harry entered the Weatherhouse he found Mr and
Mrs Brolly fast asleep in their chairs by the stove. They slept
soundly and it seemed a pity to wake them. It was so quiet
in the house that Harry could hear the old clock on the
wall ticking.

Harry could also make out another sound . . . like tinkling glass, and this sound became stronger as it went round the house. He thought he saw a shadow pass the window, but the garden just looked grey and bare and cold . . . Spring was late in coming.

Then the bag by the side of Mrs Brolly's chair began to move
and a muffled little voice said . . . "Blippy blop." It was the
little thunder cloud – wide awake and ready for a good storm.
It rose into the air and rained down on to Harry's head.

Harry began to chase the little cloud round the room, not running, but drifting and tumbling in the air. This was part of the Weatherhouse magic – if you thought you could fly, then you could – but if you were surprised, then down you came, bump!

Which is just what happened to Harry . . . He landed in a puddle made by the little thunder cloud. As he sat there he heard a voice from the garden calling softly, "Harry, Oh Harry!" . . . "Who's there?" he asked as a large card came under the door.

Harry picked up the card, but it was as cold as ice and he almost dropped it. "Mr Brolly!" he called, "We're going out to see the sparkle and fun. Won't you come too?" But Mr Brolly snored on and Mrs Brolly just murmured in her sleep.

When Harry and the little cloud went out into the garden it was still very cold and bleak.
There was no sparkle and fun anywhere!

Harry sat down on the porch steps and gazed at the bleak
garden scene. He tried to imagine how Mr Brolly would
conjure up the Spring. "Close your eyes, my boy," he would
say, "and think of happiness and sunshine." So Harry closed
his eyes.

When Harry opened his eyes, the garden was filled with sunshine. Wilkins had spread out his leaves, Bird sang on her branch and from a hole in the ground close to where Harry sat there came a sleepy sigh, a sniffle, a snuffle and a scuffling sound.

As Harry peered down the hole, he thought he could see the gleam of a pair of bright eyes . . . but he wasn't sure . . . then he heard a voice say, "It's Spring!", and the next moment a small head appeared with eyes blinking in the sunlight. It was Mole.

At the same time a soft voice said "Now the fun can begin," and Harry saw Jack Frost floating across the garden, behind him the trees were hung with icicles and the Weatherhouse windows were frosted over. Mole's nose turned blue and his teeth chattered.

"This isn't fun," said Harry shivering with cold. "But don't
worry . . . I'll make the Spring come back." Jack Frost
laughed. "My dear . . ." he said drifting closer towards Harry,
"You can't make the Spring, only the Brollys can do that."

As he drew closer to Harry, the air became colder and Harry became sleepy. It was a pleasant feeling, and he felt that he would like to curl up in a tight ball like a small animal in its burrow. "Harry! Harry, wake up," shouted Mole.

The little thunder cloud, who had seen all this from behind a
bush, gathered himself together and, rumbling furiously,
hurtled over the garden to rain on Jack Frost and melt him.
But the rain turned to frozen hail stones, and bounced
harmlessly away.

Some of the hail hit Harry on the cheek and woke him up,
and together he and the little cloud ran towards the
Weatherhouse. "Mr Brolly!" he shouted as he ran. "Blolly . . .
Blolly . . ." said the little cloud. "What is it, my boy?"
said Mr Brolly.

But before Mr Brolly could say anything more, Jack Frost
touched him with an icy finger . . . and he began to freeze.
"Brolly!" cried Mrs Brolly, "What's happening to you?" She
threw her arms around him to warm him up, but then she
too began to freeze.

"But here is the sparkle my dear," said Jack Frost. And there appeared in his hand a great diamond. "Come," he said holding out the jewel. "Take it. I made it specially for you." Harry reached up to take it, hypnotised by its cold brightness.

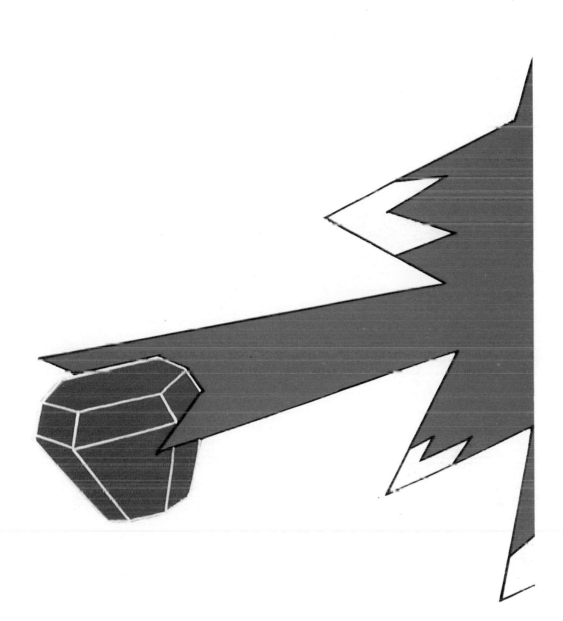

Soon they became two figures made of ice. Harry began to cry and his tears fell like shining jewels tinkling on the ground, frozen solid in the ever growing cold. "This isn't fun," he said again, "It isn't fun at all."

Harry felt his head swim and the sleepy feeling came over him again, but as his hands closed over the jewel Bird flew down from the tree, and dashed the stone to the ground. Down to the frozen earth it fell . . . and shattered into a thousand pieces.

The spell was broken, the icicles began to melt, and the colours began to return to the frozen Brollys. Jack Frost swelled and hissed with anger, and at once the drip of the icicles ceased, the air grew cold, and the Brollys began to freeze solid again.

Harry turned and ran. The garden seemed to go on forever.
On he ran, wondering what had happened to the little cloud,
until he reached the edge of a lake. Moored to a jetty was
Mr Brolly's paddle-boat. Harry started the engine, and began
to steer the boat out on to the safety of the lake.

Harry felt the boat slowing down, and saw ice in the water.
Jack Frost's laughter echoed across the lake, as the boat
froze solid. Harry watched Jack Frost gliding towards him
over the frozen lake. There was nothing to be done.

Meanwhile, the little cloud, hiding in Mrs Brolly's bag, rose up underneath the patchwork quilt like a ghost and floated out into the garden where it bumped into Mr and Mrs Brolly. The ice around them cracked and fell away from the surprised couple.

Harry, gazing out over the frozen lake, saw Mrs Brolly's quilt
coming up behind the unsuspecting Jack Frost.
Nearer and nearer it came, in all its glowing colours, and
with all its patches of planets and stars and clouds and suns.

Then . . . it fell from the sky covering Jack Frost completely. As the quilt lay flat on the deck, water began to run out from underneath. The lake water unfroze and Harry took the boat back to the jetty where he found a dripping wet Mr and Mrs Brolly.

"My boy," said Mr Brolly sneezing loudly, "How brave of you, how very bold. Mrs Brolly and I together make the Spring, but we couldn't have made it without your help. Spring is a feeling of the heart." And so saying, off he went waving his hat.

Harry woke up in his own bed, under his own patchwork quilt. He got up and looked out into the garden. Suddenly, he heard a sneeze behind him, he turned, but all he saw was Mrs Brolly standing alone, just a tiny figure made of wood . . .